CHRISTMAS EVE

AT THE

MELLOPS'

by Tomi Ungerer

Phaidon Press Limited
Regent's Wharf
All Saints Street
London, N1 9PA

Phaidon Press Inc.
180 Varick Street
New York, NY 10014

www.phaidon.com

This edition © 2011 Phaidon Press Limited
First published in German as
Familie Mellops feiert Weihnachten by Diogenes
© 1978 Diogenes Verlag AG Zürich

ISBN 978 0 7148 6250 7
002-0711

A CIP catalogue record for this book is available
from the British Library.

Printed in China

For Pam
and Michèle

One day in December Mr. Mellops read an
article in the newspaper about Christmas tree
decorations. How he loved the festive season!

With great excitement he showed the article to his sons Casimir, Isidor, Felix, and Ferdinand. "Christmas is coming!" he reminded the boys.

On Christmas Eve, Isidor decided to
surprise his father and went into the forest
to find a nice tree to decorate.

Casimir had the same idea.

Ferdinand, too, thought a tree would
be a fine surprise.

And so did Felix.

But what a to-do when they got them home! The Mellops' hall was filled with trees and tears.

"Never mind," said Mr. Mellops. "Why
don't you see if you can give your trees
away to people who don't have one yet?
And when you get back, your mother
and I will have a surprise waiting for you."

So the brothers went out into the snow. First, they decided to visit the orphanage.

When they arrived at the
orphanage all the little children
were singing happily around
a huge Christmas tree.

"Thank you very much,"
the orphans sang in harmony,
"but one tree is all we need."

So the Mellops set off for the hospital.
There, too, the patients were cheerfully
admiring their Christmas trees.

"Thank you," the patients coughed and
croaked, "but we have more trees than beds!"

Next the Mellops went to the prison.
Even there, the inmates were celebrating.
"Thank you," one prisoner mumbled
sleepily, "but I don't think there's room
in here for more than me and one tree!"

The soldiers at the town barracks were opening their gifts beside a glittering tree.

"Thank you," they cried merrily, "but we have just finished decorating our tree!"

Feeling dejected, the Mellops brothers hung
their heads. "Everyone has a Christmas tree
already," they said.

But just as they were about to give up
and throw away the trees, they came across
a little girl who was weeping quietly.

She told the brothers that she lived with
her poor grandmother who was very sick,
and she led them to her house.

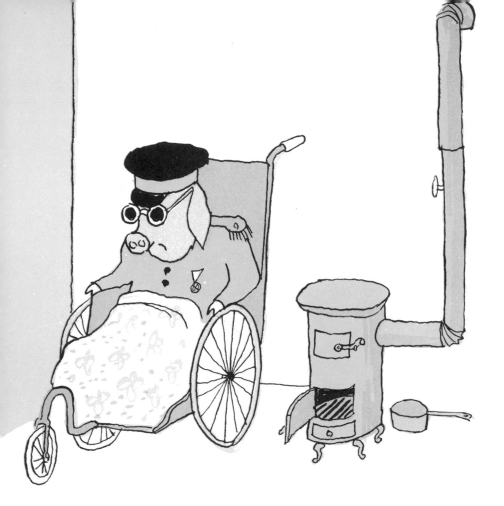

In another room of that same house
they found an old soldier, shivering
in his wheelchair.

Two frightened children huddled
alone in the attic.

And a lonely old lodger moped in
his room.

"This is where our trees are needed!"
the boys shouted.

Isidor rushed home to gather warm clothes and blankets for the people he had just met.

Felix emptied his people banks to buy them presents and medicine.

Casimir chopped wood in the forest
to heat the house.

Ferdinand filled a cart full of good
things to eat from the grocer.

The Mellops boys brought Christmas
to every room in that house.

Singing carols, the brothers made their way
home, very pleased with themselves.

Meanwhile, Mr. Mellops brought all the boys' presents
up from the cellar where they were hidden.

Mrs. Mellops decorated
the family tree...

…with shining glass balls, sugar
cookies and pretzels, tiny little toys,
and a marzipan sausage for the dog.

When the boys came home, they were
met by a wonderful sight! With cries
of delight they opened each gift.

Afterwards, Mrs. Mellops brought in a
beautiful cream cake.

"This has been the most wonderful Christmas
Eve!" announced Mr. Mellops, happily.
"I am so proud of all of you. And what's
more, I think we've learned a very important
lesson… there is no such thing as too many
Christmas trees!"